✶ONE GREAT

LOVE✶

AN ADVENT AND CHRISTMAS
✶ TREASURY OF READINGS, ✶
POEMS, AND PRAYERS

PARACLETE PRESS

PARACLETE PRESS
Brewster, Massachusetts

2022 First Printing

One Great Love: An Advent and Christmas Treasury of Readings, Poems, and Prayers

Copyright © 2022 by Paraclete Press, Inc.

ISBN 978-1-64060-796-5

The Paraclete Press name and logo (dove on cross) are trademarks of Paraclete Press

Portions of the text have been adapted for the modern audience.

COVER ART: Holly: Wayside and woodland blossoms by Edward Step | Evergreen: Köhler's Medizinal-Pflanzen | Cardinals: Mabel Osgood Wright | Bird of Jamaica: Philip Henry Gosse

    Library of Congress Cataloging-in-Publication Data
Names: Paraclete Press.
Title: One great love : an Advent and Christmas treasury of readings,
    poems, and prayers.
Description: Brewster, Massachusetts : Paraclete Press, 2022. | Summary:
    "An illustrated gift edition of inspiring and uplifting readings for the
    Advent and Christmas season"-- Provided by publisher.
Identifiers: LCCN 2022001394 (print) | LCCN 2022001395 (ebook) | ISBN
    9781640607965 (hardcover) | ISBN 9781640607972 (epub) | ISBN
    9781640607989 (pdf)
Subjects: LCSH: Advent--Miscellanea. | Christmas--Miscellanea. | Devotional
    literature.
Classification: LCC BV40 .A36 2022 (print) | LCC BV40 (ebook) | DDC
    242/.332--dc23/eng/20220210
LC record available at https://lccn.loc.gov/2022001394
LC ebook record available at https://lccn.loc.gov/2022001395

10 9 8 7 6 5 4 3 2 1

Published by Paraclete Press
Brewster, Massachusetts
www.paracletepress.com

Printed in the Republic of Korea

★ CONTENTS ★

ADVENT

O come, Desire of nations, bind
All peoples in one heart and mind;
Bid envy, strife and quarrels cease;
Fill the whole world with heaven's peace.
—*Rev. Henry Sloane Coffin, 1916, translator*

The season of Advent marks a turning from ordinary time to sacred time. In the Northern Hemisphere it comes when the hours of sunlight grow shorter and nights grow colder. The harvest has been gathered in, and a season of waiting begins.

The human mind resists waiting. We think in *Chronos* time—clock time, minute by minute, hour by hour. We order a meal from a restaurant window and expect it to be handed to us through another window only moments later. We want instant return on investments. And we expect leaders to speak in sound bites and offer quick solutions to large problems.

But God works in *Kairos* time. In God's view, "One day is with the Lord as a thousand years, and a thousand years as one day" (2 Peter 3:8). Past, present, and future are all rolled into one. So Advent breaks into the pell-mell rush of our lives and bids us to stop, look, and listen. It bids us to break free of *Chronos* time and enter *Kairos* time. It bids us to quieten our frenetic pace and perhaps linger awhile over classic words of wisdom, both ancient and new.

The dark night wakes, the glory breaks,
And Christmas comes once more.
—Phillips Brooks, 1868

As the ancients awaited a Savior who would throw off the iron yoke of oppressive world systems, "When the fulness of the time was come, God sent forth his Son" (Galatians 4:4). Not as a conquering king did the Savior come, but as a tiny baby born in a stable to a poverty-stricken, humble mother.

But this child was destined to fulfill Isaiah's promise (66:1),

The Spirit of the Lord God is upon me,
  because the Lord has anointed me
to bring good tidings to the afflicted;
  he has sent me to bind up the brokenhearted,
to proclaim liberty to the captives,
  and the opening of the prison to those who are bound.

Some of the world's great literature celebrates the birth of this child named Jesus, the one who is called *Emmanuel*, meaning "God with us."

Think of it! *God* with us. Not dwelling in some distant heaven or in a pagan temple.

God *with* us. Not reigning from an imperial throne, but come to live with us and walk alongside us throughout every ebb and flow of our lives.

God with *us*! Whoever we are, wherever we are, no matter what continent we live on or our station in life or the color of our skin, *God* has come to be *with us*.

The Nativity, Lorenzo Lotto (ca. 1480–1556/57)

As you ponder this selection of classic stories, poems, prayers, and reproductions of beautiful artwork, we invite you to step away for a moment from the rush and stress of this season and enter *Kairos* time. Let the stories touch you with their wisdom and the artworks with their beauty.

And may you experience a blessed Advent and a joy-filled Christmas!

—The Editors of Paraclete Press

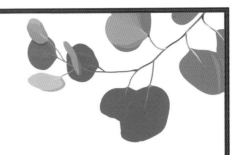

ADVENT

O COME, EMMANUEL

O come, O come, Emmanuel,
And ransom captive Israel,
That mourns in lonely exile here
Until the Son of God appear.

Rejoice! Rejoice! Emmanuel
shall come to thee, O Israel.

O come, Thou Day-spring, come and cheer
Our spirits by Thine advent here;
And drive away the shades of night
And pierce the clouds and bring us light!

Rejoice! Rejoice! Emmanuel
shall come to thee, O Israel.

O come, Thou Key of David, come,
And open wide our heavenly home;
Make safe the way that leads on high,
And close the path to misery.

Rejoice! Rejoice! Emmanuel
shall come to thee, O Israel.

O come, O come, Thou Lord of might,
Who to Thy tribes on Sinai's height
In ancient times once gave the law
In cloud, and majesty, and awe.

Rejoice! Rejoice! Emmanuel
shall come to thee, O Israel.

—SEVENTH-CENTURY LATIN HYMN,
translation by John Mason Neale (1818–1866)

11

God as Architect of the World, From: The Frontispiece of Bible Moralisee Codex Vindobonensis 2554 (French, ca. 1250), in the Österreichische Nationalbibliothek.

Hope has this lovely vowel at its throat.
Think how we cry "Oh!" as the sun's circle
clears the ridge above us on the hill.
O is the shape of a mouth singing, and of
a cherry as it lends its sweetness
to the tongue. "Oh!" say the open eyes at
unexpected beauty and then, "Wow!"
O is endless as a wedding ring, a round
pool, the shape of a drop's widening on
the water's surface. O is the center of love,
and O was in the invention of the wheel.
It multiplies in the zoo, doubles in a door
that opens, grows in the heart of a green wood,
in the moon, and in the endless looping
circuit of the planets. Mood carries it,
and books and holy fools, cotton, a useful tool
and knitting wool. I love the doubled O
in good and cosmos, and how O revolves,
solves, is in itself complete, unbroken,
a circle enclosing us, holding us all together,
every thing both in center and circumference
zeroing in on the Omega that finds
its ultimate center in the name of God.

—LUCI SHAW (1928–), *The Generosity*

13

The Annunciation, Alexander Ivanov (1806–1858)

AND THE ANGEL CAME TO MARY AND SAID, "Hail, O favored one, the Lord is with you."

But she was greatly troubled at the saying, and considered in her mind what sort of greeting this might be.

And the angel said to her, "Do not be afraid, Mary, for you have found favor with God. And behold, you will conceive in your womb and bear a son, and you shall call his name Jesus. He will be great, and will be called the Son of the Most High; and the Lord God will give to him the throne of his father David, and he will reign over the house of Jacob for ever; and of his kingdom there will be no end."

And Mary said to the angel, "How shall this be, since I have no husband?"

And the angel said to her, "The Holy Spirit will come upon you, and the power of the Most High will overshadow you; therefore the child to be born will be called holy, the Son of God. And behold, your kinswoman Elizabeth in her old age has also conceived a son; and this is the sixth month with her who was called barren. For with God nothing will be impossible."

And Mary said, "Behold, I am the handmaid of the Lord; let it be to me according to your word."

And the angel departed from her.

—LUKE 1:28–38 (RSV), ADAPTED

I'm a sucker for
those tales of origin
where the hero or heroine
comes to life on
the wrong side of the tracks.
The storyteller speeds us back
to the site of shack, or hovel
or humble village
like, say, Nazareth.
Here, the Heaven Express
makes a single stop
and out steps The Messenger
wings neatly folded away
brightness his only uniform.
Our heroine is immediately
distracted by his greeting
and why wouldn't she be?
Seriously, who in his right mind
would call anyone living in
a penny-ante town like Nazareth
blessed or favored?
And yet Gabriel
called her favored twice
lest anyone forget.

Oh, the Gabriel–Mary encounter
is certainly well known
but it's the details
we need pay attention to.
What made Mary favored
in the first place?
Was it perhaps that she was ready
to bear the impossible
to carry the Christ inside her
no matter the cost?
And are we ready to do the same?
If so, by God's grace
we each wear this soul's tattoo:
Favored one.
And we get to carry
the Christmas gift
of the Lord's Light
wherever there is sunrise.

Luke 1:26–38

—Nikki Grimes (1950–), *Glory in the Margins*

The Annunciation, Church of Our Lady of the Assumption. Cordon.
Haute-Savoie. France.

Mark the season of Advent by loving and serving others with God's own love and concern.

—St. Mother Teresa (1910–1997)

★ CHRISTMAS GIFTS ★

JO WAS THE FIRST TO WAKE IN THE GRAY DAWN of Christmas morning. No stockings hung at the fireplace, and for a moment she felt as much disappointed as she did long ago, when her little sock fell down because it was so crammed with goodies. Then she remembered her mother's promise, and slipping her hand under her pillow, drew out a little crimson-covered book. She knew it very well, for it was that beautiful old story of the best life ever lived, and Jo felt that it was a true guide-book for any pilgrim going the long journey. She woke Meg with a "Merry Christmas," and bade her see what was under her pillow. A green-covered book appeared, with the same picture inside, and a few words written by their mother, which made their one present very precious in their eyes. Presently Beth and Amy woke, to rummage and find their little books also,—one dove-colored, the other blue; and all sat looking at and talking about them, while the East grew rosy with the coming day.

In spite of her small vanities, Margaret had a sweet and pious nature, which unconsciously influenced her sisters, especially Jo, who loved her very tenderly, and obeyed her because her advice was so gently given.

"Girls," said Meg, seriously, looking from the tumbled head beside her to the two little night-capped ones in the room beyond, "mother wants us to read and love and mind these books, and we must begin at once. We used to be faithful about it; but since father went away, and all this war trouble unsettled us, we have neglected many things. You can do as you please; but *I* shall keep my book on the table here, and read a little every morning as soon as I wake, for I know it will do me good, and help me through the day."

20

Then she opened her new book and began to read. Jo put her arm round her, and, leaning cheek to cheek, read also, with the quiet expression so seldom seen on her restless face.

"How good Meg is! Come, Amy, let's do as they do. I'll help you with the hard words, and they'll explain things if we don't understand," whispered Beth, very much impressed by the pretty books and her sisters' example.

"I'm glad mine is blue," said Amy; and then the rooms were very still while the pages were softly turned, and the winter sunshine crept in to touch the bright heads and serious faces with a Christmas greeting.

"Where is mother?" asked Meg, as she and Jo ran down to thank her for their gifts, half an hour later.

"Goodness only knows. Some poor person come a-beggin', and your ma went straight off to see what was needed. There never *was* such a woman for givin' away vittles and drink, clothes and firin'," replied Hannah, who had lived with the family since Meg was born, and was considered by them all more as a friend than a housekeeper.

"She will be back soon, I guess; so do your cakes, and have everything ready," said Meg, looking over the presents which were collected in a basket and kept under the sofa, ready to be produced at the proper time. "Why, where is Amy's bottle of Cologne?" she added, as the little flask did not appear.

"She took it out a minute ago, and went off with it to put a ribbon on it, or some such notion," replied Jo, dancing about the room to take the first stiffness off the new army-slippers.

"How nice my handkerchiefs look, don't they? Hannah washed and ironed them for me, and I marked them all myself," said Beth, looking proudly at the somewhat uneven letters which had cost her such labor.

"Bless the child, she's gone and put 'Mother' on them instead of 'M. March;' how funny!" cried Jo, taking up one.

"Isn't it right? I thought it was better to do it so, because Meg's initials are 'M. M.,' and I don't want any one to use these but Marmee," said Beth, looking troubled.

"It's all right, dear, and a very pretty idea; quite sensible, too, for no one can ever mistake now. It will please her very much, I know," said Meg, with a frown for Jo, and a smile for Beth.

"There's mother; hide the basket, quick!" cried Jo, as a door slammed, and steps sounded in the hall.

Amy came in hastily, and looked rather abashed when she saw her sisters all waiting for her.

"Where have you been, and what are you hiding behind you?" asked Meg, surprised to see, by her hood and cloak, that lazy Amy had been out so early.

"Don't laugh at me, Jo, I didn't mean any one should know till the time came. I only meant to change the little bottle for a big one, and I gave *all* my money to get it, and I'm truly trying not to be selfish any more."

As she spoke. Amy showed the handsome flask which replaced the cheap one; and looked so earnest and humble in her little effort to forget herself, that Meg hugged her on the spot, and Jo pronounced her "a trump," while Beth ran to the window, and picked her finest rose to ornament the stately bottle.

"You see I felt ashamed of my present, after reading and talking about being good this morning, so I ran round the corner and changed it the minute I was up; and I'm *so* glad, for mine is the handsomest now."

Another bang of the street-door sent the basket under the sofa, and the girls to the table eager for breakfast.

"Merry Christmas, Marmee! Lots of them! Thank you for our books; we read some, and mean to every day," they cried, in chorus.

"Merry Christmas, little daughters! I'm glad you began at once, and hope you will keep on. But I want to say one word before we sit down. Not far away from here lies a poor woman with a little new-born baby. Six children are huddled into one bed to keep from freezing, for they have no fire. There is nothing to eat over there; and the oldest boy came to tell me they were suffering hunger and cold. My girls, will you give them your breakfast as a Christmas present?"

They were all unusually hungry, having waited nearly an hour, and for a minute no one spoke; only a minute, for Jo exclaimed impetuously,—

"I'm so glad you came before we began!"

"May I go and help carry the things to the poor little children?" asked Beth, eagerly.

"*I* shall take the cream and the muffins," added Amy, heroically giving up the articles she most liked.

Meg was already covering the buckwheats, and piling the bread into one big plate.

"I thought you'd do it," said Mrs. March, smiling as if satisfied. "You shall all go and help me, and when we come back we will have bread and milk for breakfast, and make it up at dinnertime."

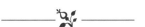

"Not far away from here lies a poor woman with a little new-born baby. Six children are huddled into one bed to keep from freezing, for they have no fire. There is nothing to eat over there; and the oldest boy came to tell me they were suffering hunger and cold. My girls, will you give them your breakfast as a Christmas present?"

They were soon ready, and the procession set out. Fortunately it was early, and they went through back streets, so few people saw them, and no one laughed at the funny party.

A poor, bare, miserable room it was, with broken windows, no fire, ragged bed-clothes, a sick mother, wailing baby, and a group of pale, hungry children cuddled under one old quilt, trying to keep warm. How the big eyes stared, and the blue lips smiled, as the girls went in!

"*Ach, mein Gott!* it is good angels come to us!" cried the poor woman, crying for joy.

"Funny angels in hoods and mittens," said Jo, and set them laughing.

In a few minutes it really did seem as if kind spirits had been at work there. Hannah, who had carried wood, made a fire, and stopped up the broken panes with old hats, and her own shawl. Mrs. March gave the mother tea and gruel, and comforted her with promises of help, while she dressed the little baby as tenderly as if it had been her own. The girls, meantime, spread the table, set the children round the fire, and fed them like so many hungry birds; laughing, talking, and trying to understand the funny broken English.

"*Das ist gute!*" "*Der angel-kinder!*" cried the poor things, as they ate, and warmed their purple hands at the comfortable blaze. The girls had never been called angel children before, and thought it very agreeable, especially Jo. That was a very happy breakfast, though they didn't get any of it; and when they went away, leaving comfort behind, I think there were not in all the city four merrier people than the hungry little girls who gave away their breakfasts, and contented themselves with bread and milk on Christmas morning.

"That's loving our neighbor better than ourselves, and I like it," said Meg, as they set out their presents, while their mother was up stairs collecting clothes for the poor Hummels.

Not a very splendid show, but there was a great deal of love done up in the few little bundles; and the tall vase of red roses, white chrysanthemums, and trailing vines, which stood in the middle, gave quite an elegant air to the table.

"She's coming! strike up, Beth, open the door, Amy. Three cheers for Marmee!" cried Jo, prancing about, while Meg went to conduct mother to the seat of honor.

Beth played her gayest march, Amy threw open the door, and Meg enacted escort with great dignity. Mrs. March was both surprised and touched; and smiled with her eyes full as she examined her presents, and read the little notes which accompanied them. The slippers went on at once, a new handkerchief was slipped into her pocket, well scented with Amy's Cologne, the rose was fastened in her bosom, and the nice gloves were pronounced "a perfect fit."

There was a good deal of laughing, and kissing, and explaining, in the simple, loving fashion which makes these home-festivals so pleasant at the time, so sweet to remember long afterward.

There was a good deal of laughing, and kissing, and explaining, in the simple, loving fashion which makes these home-festivals so pleasant at the time, so sweet to remember long afterward, and then all fell to work.

The morning charities and ceremonies took so much time, that the rest of the day was devoted to preparations for the evening festivities. Being still too young to go often to the theatre, and not rich enough to afford any great outlay for private performances, the girls put their wits to work, and, necessity being the mother of invention, made whatever they needed.

—Louisa May Alcott (1832–1888), *Little Women*

COME, THOU
★ LONG EXPECTED JESUS ★

Come, thou long expected Jesus,
born to set thy people free;
from our fears and sins release us,
let us find our rest in thee.
Israel's strength and consolation,
hope of all the earth thou art;
dear desire of every nation,
joy of every longing heart.

27

Born thy people to deliver,
born a child and yet a King,
born to reign in us forever,
now thy gracious kingdom bring.
By thine own eternal spirit
rule in all our hearts alone;
by thine all sufficient merit,
raise us to thy glorious throne.

—CHARLES WESLEY (1707–1788)

BIRTH: WONDER . . . ASTONISHMENT . . . ADORATION. There can't be very many of us for whom the sheer fact of existence hasn't rocked us back on our heels. We take off our sandals before the burning bush. We catch our breath at the sight of a plummeting hawk. "Thank you, God." We find ourselves in a lavish existence in which we feel a deep sense of kinship—we *belong* here; we say thanks with our lives to Life. And not just "Thanks" or "Thank It" but "Thank *You*." Most of the people who have lived on this planet earth have identified this You with God or gods. This is not just a matter of learning our manners, the way children are taught to say thank you as a social grace. It is the cultivation of adequateness within ourselves to the nature of reality, developing the capacity to sustain an adequate response to the overwhelming gift and goodness of life.

Wonder is the only adequate launching pad for exploring this fullness, this whole-ness, of human life. Once a year, each Christmas, for a few days at least, we and millions of our neighbors turn aside from our preoccupations with life reduced to biology or economics or psychology and join together in a community of wonder. The wonder keeps us open-eyed, expectant, alive to life that is always more than we can account for, that always exceeds our calculations, that is always beyond anything we can make.

Wonder is the only adequate launching pad for exploring this fullness, this wholeness, of human life.

If in the general festive round of singing and decorating, giving and receiving, cooking meals and family gatherings, we ask what is behind all this and what keeps it going all over the world, among all classes of people quite regardless of whether they believe or not, the answer is simply "a birth." Not just "birth" in general, but a particular birth in a small Middle Eastern village in datable time—a named baby, Jesus—a birth that soon had people talking and singing about God, indeed, *worshiping* God.

This invites reflection. For birth, simply as birth, even though often enough greeted with wonder and accompanied with ceremony and celebration, has a way of getting absorbed into business as usual far too soon. The initial impulses of gratitude turn out to be astonishingly ephemeral. Birth in itself does not seem to compel belief in God. There are plenty of people who take each new life on its own terms and deal with the person just as he or she comes to us, no questions asked. There is something very attractive about this: it is so clean and uncomplicated and noncontroversial. And obvious. They get a satisfying sense of the inherently divine in life itself without all the complications of church: the theology, the mess of church history, the hypocrisies of church-goers, the incompetence of pastors, the appeals for money. Life, as life, seems perfectly capable of furnishing them with a spirituality that exults in beautiful beaches and fine sunsets, surfing and skiing and body massage, emotional states and aesthetic titillation without investing too much God-attentiveness in a baby.

But for all its considerable attractions, this shift of attention from birth to aspects of the world that please us on our terms is considerably deficient in person. Birth means that a *person* is alive in the world. A miracle of sorts, to be sure, but a miracle that very soon gets obscured by late-night feedings, diapers, fevers, and inconvenient irruptions of fussiness and squalling. Soon the realization sets in that we are in for years and years of the child's growing-up time that will stretch our stamina and patience, sometimes to the breaking point.

So how did it happen that *this* birth, this *Jesus* birth managed to set so many of us back on our heels in astonishment and gratitude and wonder? And continues to do so century after century, at least at this time of year?

The brief answer is that this wasn't just any birth. The baby's parents and first witnesses were convinced that God was entering human history in human form. Their conviction was confirmed in angel and Magi and shepherds visitations; eventually an extraordinary life came into being before their eyes, right in their neighborhood. More and more people became convinced. Men, women, and children from all over the world continue to be convinced right up to the present moment.

Birth, every human birth, is an occasion for local wonder. In Jesus' birth the wonder is extrapolated across the screen of all creation and all history as a God-birth. "The Word became flesh and dwelt among us"—moved into the neighborhood, so to speak. And for thirty years or so, men and women saw God in speech and action in the entirely human person of Jesus as he was subject, along with them, to the common historical conditions of, as Charles Williams once put it, "Jewish religion, Roman order, and Greek intellect." These were not credulous people and it was not easy for them to believe, but they did. That God was made incarnate as a human baby is still not easy to believe, but people continue to do so. Many, even those who don't "believe," find themselves happy to participate in the giving and receiving, singing and celebrating of those who do.

Incarnation, *in-flesh-ment,* God in human form in Jesus entering our history: this is what started Christmas. This is what keeps Christmas going.

—Eugene Peterson (1932–2018),
God With Us: Rediscovering the Meaning of Christmas

Young Peasant at Her Toilette, Camille Pissarro (1830–1903)

Thy cradle here shall glitter bright,
And darkness breathe a newer light,
Where endless faith shall shine serene,
And twilight never intervene.
All laud to God the Father be,
All praise, eternal Son, to Thee;
All glory, as is ever meet,
To God the Holy Paraclete.

—St. Ambrose of Milan (340–397),
translation by John Mason Neale (1818–1866)

32

"Be still, and know that I am God.
I am exalted among the nations,
I am exalted in the earth!"
The Lord of hosts is with us;
the God of Jacob is our refuge.

—Psalm 46:10–11 (rsv)

Star of the Hero, Nicholas Roerich (1874–1947)

For outlandish creatures like us, on our way to a heart, a brain, and courage, Bethlehem is not the end of our journey but only the beginning—not home but the place through which we must pass if ever we are to reach home at last.

—FREDERICK BUECHNER (1926–)

34

The Ferryman, Jean-Baptiste-Camille Corot (1796–1875)

WAITING SHAPES MUCH OF
✳ OUR LIVES ✳

WAITING IS A FUNDAMENTAL PART OF OUR LIVES. We often find ourselves waiting. We all know what it is like to wait for someone we expect to come, often becoming quite impatient until they finally arrive. Or we find ourselves waiting for a call and looking at our watches as we hope to hear the phone ring; after all, we'd agreed on a time to talk. And we often find ourselves waiting in lines at a store, a bus stop, or in airport security lines that stand between us and making our flight on time. Waiting shapes much of our lives. And, to be honest, we often find it hard to wait, especially in circumstances over which we have little control. Advent is a time of waiting, a season of expectation when we learn how to wait for God's coming into our hearts—again and again. In these weeks, we know in our hearts that when God does come all will be well and we will experience what it means to come home to ourselves. We have just this experience when we give ourselves to those longings of our heart that reach beyond this world, and when we come to see that, we do have the strength to wait. For it is in this waiting that we come to know our true self; in this experience, we feel ourselves becoming one in the moment. We discover a quiet center within ourselves, and realize that this moment holds everything that is important for us. We are simply here, now, in this moment—aware, attentive, and present.

Pay particular attention, throughout the day, to times when you find yourself waiting—for an elevator, for a bus or subway, in a line at the store, in traffic congestion, for a guest to arrive. In such moments, pay attention to what it means to wait—with expectation. Attend to your impatience, saying quietly to yourself: It really is not that important when I arrive. Give yourself fully to this moment, and seek to rest within yourself. Say to yourself: "I'm not just waiting for the bus; I'm waiting for God, who is already present in my life. I'm waiting for the Lord who wants me to welcome him, and who will come when I am truly present." If you sense your own impatience, give it to God. When you do this, you'll find yourself becoming quiet in your heart and begin to sense God protecting you. You'll start to feel yourself becoming free of the pressure of fulfilling others' expectations. In this moment, give your waiting and even your impatience to God. In doing so, you'll begin to find your discomfort fade away. A newfound patience will bring new energy and aliveness to you.

—ANSELM GRÜN (1945–), *Your Light Gives Us Hope,*
translation by Mark S. Burrows (1955–)

The Wait, Toivo Santeri Salokivi (1886–1940)

Ere by the spheres time was created, thou
Wast in His mind, who is thy Son and Brother;
Whom thou conceivst, conceived; yea thou art now
Thy Maker's maker, and thy Father's mother;
Thou hast light in dark, and shuts in little room,
Immensity cloistered in thy dear womb.

—JOHN DONNE (1572–1631)

38

The Belles Heures of Jean de France, duc de Berry,
The Limbourg Brothers (1405–1408/1409)

Young Mary, loitering once her garden way,
Felt a warm splendor grow in the April day,
As wine that blushes water through. And soon,
Out of the gold air of the afternoon,
One knelt before her: hair he had, or fire,
Bound back above his ears with golden wire,
Baring the eager marble of his face.
Not man's nor woman's was the immortal grace
Rounding the limbs beneath that robe of white,
And lighting the proud eyes with changeless light,
Incurious. Calm as his wings, and fair,
That presence filled the garden.

    She stood there,
Saying, "What would you, Sir?"
    He told his word,
"Blessed art thou of women!" Half she heard,
Hands folded and face bowed, half long had known,
The message of that clear and holy tone,
That fluttered hot sweet sobs about her heart;
Such serene tidings moved such human smart.
Her breath came quick as little flakes of snow.
Her hands crept up her breast. She did but know
It was not hers. She felt a trembling stir
Within her body, a will too strong for her
That held and filled and mastered all. With eyes
Closed, and a thousand soft short broken sighs,
She gave submission; fearful, meek, and glad.

39

She wished to speak. Under her breasts she had
Such multitudinous burnings, to and fro,
And throbs not understood; she did not know
If they were hurt or joy for her; but only
That she was grown strange to herself, half lonely,
All wonderful, filled full of pains to come
And thoughts she dare not think, swift thoughts and dumb,
Human, and quaint, her own, yet very far,
Divine, dear, terrible, familiar . . .
Her heart was faint for telling; to relate
Her limbs' sweet treachery, her strange high estate,
Over and over, whispering, half revealing,
Weeping; and so find kindness to her healing.
'Twixt tears and laughter, panic hurrying her,
She raised her eyes to that fair messenger.
He knelt unmoved, immortal; with his eyes
Gazing beyond her, calm to the calm skies;
Radiant, untroubled in his wisdom, kind.
His sheaf of lilies stirred not in the wind.
How should she, pitiful with mortality,
Try the wide peace of that felicity
With ripples of her perplexed shaken heart,
And hints of human ecstasy, human smart,
And whispers of the lonely weight she bore,
And how her womb within was hers no more
And at length hers?

    Being tired, she bowed her head;
And said, "So be it!"

The great wings were spread
Showering glory on the fields, and fire.
The whole air, singing, bore him up, and higher,
Unswerving, unreluctant. Soon he shone
A gold speck in the gold skies; then was gone.

The air was colder, and grey. She stood alone.

—RUPERT BROOKE (1887–1915)

41

THE ENGLISH WORD FOR ADVENT COMES FROM THE Latin word *adventus*: coming, approach, arrival. But the season of Advent is more than that. Of course, the arrival is key to Advent, after all, what would be the point of Advent if there was no arrival of Christ to mark the end? But what do we do in the meantime? What happens between the beginning of December and Christmas day? We wait.

The origin of the English word for *wait* comes from an Old French word meaning a watcher, an onlooker, a sentry of sorts. It is not the season of sitting back, like a child fidgeting as they wait for their parents. We do not sit back on our heels, bored at the thought of killing more time. There is nothing passive about the waiting of Advent. It is not a break, not a chance to catch our breath. It is the time to be aware, to be hyperconscious of the goings-on around us, to be ever attentive to signs and wonders that may otherwise escape our notice. After all, the Messiah was born in a dirty stable, in an overcrowded village, hardly noticed in the hubbub of his day. We must be vigilant, like guards in the night, searching through the darkness to find the light, for we do not want the Messiah to pass unnoticed again.

The Latin word *sperare* modernized into Spanish as *esperar* and French as *espérer*. The Spanish and the French words have similar meanings: to wait for, and to expect, respectively. The French adds another layer to the waiting of Advent. Not only are we attentive sentries, searching in the dark, but we are *expecting* the coming of Christ. It is not a fruitless search, but a vigilant watch for an expected guest. The Spanish word also has a second meaning of "to hope for."

Hope can be a vague concept, ill-defined, and often misused. A secular definition of Hope is "to cherish a desire with anticipation."

Seems fitting for Advent. An archaic definition for hope equals it to trust. To go further, Hebrews 11:1 defines the intangible web of hope and faith as "[faith] is the substance of things hoped for, the evidence of things not seen." The light of Christ is hope realized. Saint Paul goes further to reassure us in Romans 5:5, "Now hope does not disappoint because the love of God has been poured out in our hearts by the Holy Spirit who was given to us."

If we follow the Spanish, not only will we be waiting in the cold, dark night of winter, but we will be hoping, expecting with confidence, wholly trusting in the arrival of Christ. This is fitting, as the Latin word *sperare* literally means "to hope."

. . . we will be hoping, expecting with confidence, wholly trusting in the arrival of Christ.

What do we want to hold with us this Advent? Will we be overrun by the overwhelming consumerism that seems to only grow more rampant in each passing year? Will we sit back, tiredly waiting as another present, another party, another plasticly perfect creche scene passes us by? Or will we ever attentively watch, hope, expect, and trust in the return of Christ?

—Joy L. Carter (1991–)

"Everything that is worthwhile must be waited for."
—Carlo Carretto (1910–1988)

Annunciation, Mikhail Nesterov (1862–1942)

44

At the break of Christmas Day,
   Through the frosty starlight ringing,
Faint and sweet and far away,
   Comes the sound of children, singing,
     Chanting, singing,
   "Cease to mourn,
   For Christ is born,
     Peace and joy to all men bringing!"

Careless that the chill winds blow,
   Growing stronger, sweeter, clearer,
Noiseless footfalls in the snow,
   Bring the happy voices nearer;
     Hear them singing,
   "Winter's drear,
   But Christ is here,
     Mirth and gladness with Him bringing."

"Merry Christmas!" hear them say,
   As the East is growing lighter;
"May the joy of Christmas Day
   Make your whole year gladder, brighter!"
     Join their singing,
   "To each home
   Our Christ has come,
     All Love's treasures with Him bringing!"

—MARGARET DELAND (1857–1945)

45

46

The people who walked in darkness
   have seen a great light;
those who dwelt in a land of deep darkness,
   on them has light shined.
Thou hast multiplied the nation,
   thou hast increased its joy;
they rejoice before thee
   as with joy at the harvest. . . .
For to us a child is born,
   to us a son is given;
and the government will be upon his shoulder,
   and his name will be called
"Wonderful Counselor, Mighty God,
   Everlasting Father, Prince of Peace."
Of the increase of his government and of peace
   there will be no end,
upon the throne of David, and over his kingdom,
   to establish it, and to uphold it
with justice and with righteousness
   from this time forth and for evermore.
The zeal of the LORD of hosts will do this.

—ISAIAH 9:2–7 (RSV), ADAPTED

The Light, Vilmos Aba-Novák (1894–1941)

The Presentation of Christ in the Temple, Giuseppe Cesari (1568–1640)

"The Lord is coming, always coming.
When you have ears to hear and eyes to see,
you will recognize him at any moment of your life.
Life is Advent;
life is recognizing the coming of the Lord."
—HENRI NOUWEN (1932–1996)

49

PRAYER IS A KIND OF AWARENESS, A COMING INTO the present moment and finding God there. It's an awareness that sees God present, here and now. We talk about Advent as a time of waiting and watching. That means it can also be about savoring the moment. It means not jumping ahead, but appreciating what is before us.

50

But waiting can be such a hard thing. We're not good at waiting, and we can see how our impatience affects different areas of life. When people tell me they feel impatient with others, I sometimes ask if they feel impatient with themselves, too. The answer is usually yes. When we're not patient with ourselves, when we don't allow ourselves to be imperfect and finite, or don't give ourselves time to learn and grow—it shows in the way we treat others.

Our impatience extends to Advent, too. Are you ready for Christmas when it comes, or are you feeling fed up by December 26, when the celebrating should really be getting started? When I was a kid, I remember getting an Advent calendar, one with the little doors that you open on each day leading up to Christmas. What a nice way to encourage being "present to the present of the present." For me, though, that was asking way too much. All those doors were open long before Christmas!

The great irony: The more impatient we are, unable to wait, the more unsatisfied we are in the long term. But the more we are able to cultivate patience, the more fulfilled we are in the short term and long term. Each day has its "present." We need to be alive now, to live fully in the present, so that when Christmas comes, we'll really taste it.

—MARK A. VILLANO (1960–), *Time to Get Ready*

Waiting, Nicholas Roerich (1874–1947)

A Road in Louveciennes, Auguste Renoir (1841–1919)

As it is written in the book of the words of
Isaiah the prophet:
"A voice of one calling in the wilderness,
'Prepare the way for the Lord,
make straight paths for him.'"

—Luke 3:4 (NIV)

The farm has not changed.
Its Christmas windows welcomed me
when I was two feet smaller.
The granddaughter of the first collie I knew
bounces out to meet me, a flow of black and white.

We are all of us older
but the hands are no less warm;
the friendship and talk as rich,
as precious as in the beginning –
the hills in the window will always remain.

—Kenneth Steven (1968–), *Iona*

53

The Shepherds.
Where the humble shepherds waking,
Kept their guard throughout the night;
Suddenly the heavens breaking,
Poured around them glorious light;
Then an Angel quick descended,
Clothed in holy majesty,
While the men with awe attended;
And amazed at what they see,
Hear the angel's exhortation;
"Fear ye not, for Joy I bring,
Tidings of the world's Salvation,
Of the Birth of Israel's King:
"In a manger lying lowly,
In the City, where of old
Royal David, pure and holy,
Watched o'er his father's fold:
"Where the beasts around are stalled,
Ye shall find the Newly-born,
Him, who Christ the Lord is called,
Bringer of a glorious morn."
Scarcely had the Angel ended
These sweet words of comforting,

54

When a heavenly host descended,
And with joy their praises sing;
"Unto God, who in the heaven
Dwells, be everlasting praise;
Peace on earth to man be given,
And good will through all his days."
When the men had heard the greeting,
As the angels went away,
Each began with bosom beating,
To his neighbour thus to say;
"Let us seek the lowly dwelling,
Where amid the lowing beasts,
As we heard the angels telling,
The Saviour of the world now rests.

—JOHN STANLEY TUTE (1823–1897)

55

Mountain Landscape with Shepherd, Thomas Gainsborough (1727–1788)

Little Lamb who made thee?
Dost thou know who made thee?
Gave thee life and bid thee feed
By the stream and o'er the mead;
Gave thee clothing of delight,
Softest clothing wooly bright;
Gave thee such a tender voice,
Making all the vales rejoice:
Little Lamb who made thee?
Dost thou know who made thee?

Little Lamb I'll tell thee,
Little Lamb I'll tell thee:
He is called by thy name,
For he calls himself a Lamb:
He is meek and he is mild,
He became a little child:
I a child and thou a lamb,
We are called by his name:
Little Lamb God bless thee.
Little Lamb God bless thee.

—WILLIAM BLAKE (1757–1827)

I sing of a maiden
That is matchless,
King of all kings
For her son she chose.

58

He came as still
Where his mother was
As dew in April
That falls on the grass.

He came as still
To his mother's bower
As dew in April
That falls on the flower.

He came as still
Where his mother lay
As dew in April
That falls on the spray.

Mother and maiden
There was never, ever one but she;
Well may such a lady
God's mother be.

—FOURTEENTH-CENTURY HYMN

The Immaculate Conception, Alonzo Cano (1601–1667)

"My soul magnifies the Lord,

And my spirit has rejoiced in God my Savior.

For He has regarded the lowly state of His maidservant;

For behold, henceforth all generations will call me blessed.

For He who is mighty has done great things for me,

And holy is His name.

And His mercy is on those who fear Him

From generation to generation.

He has shown strength with His arm;

He has scattered the proud in the imagination of their hearts.

He has put down the mighty from their thrones,

And exalted the lowly.

He has filled the hungry with good things,

And the rich He has sent away empty.

He has helped His servant Israel,

In remembrance of His mercy,

As He spoke to our fathers,

To Abraham and to his seed forever."

—LUKE 1:46–55 (NKJV), ADAPTED

Do you see this grain of sand
Lying loosely in my hand?
Do you know to me it brought
Just a simple loving thought?
When one gazes night by night
On the glorious stars of light,
Oh how little seems the span
Measured round the life of man.

Oh! how fleeting are his years
With their smiles and their tears;
Can it be that God does care
For such atoms as we are?
Then outspake this grain of sand
"I was fashioned by His hand
In the star lit realms of space
I was made to have a place."

Should the ocean flood the world,
Were its mountains 'gainst me hurled
All the force they could employ
Wouldn't a single grain destroy;
And if I, a thing so light,
Have a place within His sight;
You are linked unto his throne
Cannot live nor die alone.

—Frances Ellen Watkins Harper (1825–1911)

Oak Fractured by a Lightning, Maxim Vorobiev (1787–1855)

"The dying words of Goethe."

"Light! more light! the shadows deepen,
    And my life is ebbing low,
Throw the windows widely open:
    Light! more light! before I go.

"Softly let the balmy sunshine
    Play around my dying bed,
E'er the dimly lighted valley
    I with lonely feet must tread.

"Light! more light! for Death is weaving
    Shadows 'round my waning sight,
And I fain would gaze upon him
    Through a stream of earthly light."

Not for greater gifts of genius;
    Not for thoughts more grandly bright,
All the dying poet whispers
    Is a prayer for light, more light.

Heeds he not the gathered laurels,
    Fading slowly from his sight;
All the poet's aspirations
    Centre in that prayer for light.

64

Gracious Saviour, when life's day-dreams
Melt and vanish from the sight,
May our dim and longing vision
Then be blessed with light, more light.

—FRANCES ELLEN WATKINS HARPER (1825–1911)

CHRISTMAS

LOVE CAME DOWN

LET US GO IN HEART AND MIND
✴ TO BETHLEHEM ✴

Beloved in Christ,
this Christmastide, it is our duty and delight
to prepare ourselves to hear again the message of the angels,
and to go in heart and mind to Bethlehem,
and see this thing which is come to pass,
and the Babe lying in a manger.

Therefore let us hear again from Holy Scripture
the tale of the loving purposes of God from the first days of
    our sin
until the glorious redemption brought us by this holy Child;
and let us make this house of prayer glad with our carols of
    praise.

But first, because this of all things would rejoice Jesus' heart,
let us pray to him for the needs of the whole world, and all
    his people;
for peace upon the earth he came to save;
for love and unity within the one Church he did build;
for goodwill among all peoples.

And particularly at this time let us remember
the poor, the cold, the hungry, the oppressed;
the sick and them that mourn; the lonely and the unloved;
the aged and the little children;

Lastly, let us remember all those who rejoice with us,
but upon another shore and in a greater light,
that multitude which no one can number,
whose hope was in the Word made flesh,
and with whom, in this Lord Jesus, we for evermore are one.

—ERIC MILNER-WHITE (1884–1963)

68

★ AVE MARIS STELLA ★

Hail, bright star of ocean,
God's own Mother blest,
Ever sinless Virgin,
Gate of heavenly rest.

Taking that sweet Ave
Which from Gabriel came,
Peace confirm within us,
Changing Eva's name.

69

Break the captives' fetters,
Light on blindness pour,
All our ills expelling,
Every bliss implore.

Show thyself a Mother;
May the Word Divine,
Born for us thy Infant,
Hear our prayers through thine.

Virgin all excelling,
Mildest of the mild,
Freed from guilt, preserve us,
Pure and undefiled.

Keep our life all spotless,
Make our way secure,
Till we find in Jesus,
Joy forevermore.

Through the highest heaven
To the Almighty Three,
Father, Son and Spirit,
One same glory be. Amen.

—St. Bernard of Clairvaux (1090–1153)

70

Madonna of the Fir Tree, Marianne Preindelsberger Stokes (1855–1927)

ARE YOU WILLING TO
★ STOOP DOWN? ★

ARE YOU WILLING TO STOOP DOWN AND CONSIDER the needs and desires of little children; to remember the weaknesses and loneliness of people who are growing old; to stop asking how much your friends love you, and to ask yourself if you love them enough; to bear in mind the things that other people have to bear on their hearts; to trim your lamp so that it will give more light and less smoke, and to carry it in front so that your shadow will fall behind you; to make a grave for your ugly thoughts and a garden for your kindly feelings, with the gate open? Are you willing to do these things for a day? Then you are ready to keep Christmas!

—HENRY VAN DYKE (1852–1933)

The Carols, Nikiforos Lytras (1832–1904)

PAPA PANOV'S
★ SPECIAL CHRISTMAS ★

IT WAS CHRISTMAS EVE AND ALTHOUGH IT WAS still afternoon, lights had begun to appear in the shops and houses of the little Russian village, for the short winter day was nearly over. Excited children scurried indoors and now only muffled sounds of chatter and laughter escaped from closed shutters.

Old Papa Panov, the village shoemaker, stepped outside his shop to take one last look around. The sounds of happiness, the bright lights, and the faint but delicious smells of Christmas cooking reminded him of past Christmas times when his wife had still been alive and his own children little. Now they had gone. His usually cheerful face, with the little laughter wrinkles behind the round steel spectacles, looked sad now. But he went back indoors with a firm step, put up the shutters and set a pot of coffee to heat on the charcoal stove. Then, with a sigh, he settled in his big armchair.

Papa Panov did not often read, but tonight he pulled down the big old family Bible and, slowly tracing the lines with one forefinger, he read again the Christmas story. He read how Mary and Joseph, tired by their journey to Bethlehem, found no room for them at the inn, so that Mary's little baby was born in the cowshed.

"Oh, dear, oh, dear!" exclaimed Papa Panov, "if only they had come here! I would have given them my bed and I could have covered the baby with my patchwork quilt to keep him warm."

He read on about the wise men who had come to see the baby Jesus, bringing him splendid gifts. Papa Panov's face fell. "I have no gift that I could give him," he thought sadly.

Then his face brightened. He put down the Bible, got up and stretched his long arms to the shelf high up in his little room. He took down a small, dusty box and opened it. Inside was a perfect pair of tiny leather shoes. Papa Panov smiled with satisfaction. Yes, they were as good as he had remembered—the best shoes he had ever made. "I should give him those," he decided, as he gently put them away and sat down again.

He was feeling tired now, and the further he read the sleepier he became. The print began to dance before his eyes so that he closed them, just for a minute. In no time at all Papa Panov was fast asleep.

And as he slept he dreamed. He dreamed that someone was in his room and he knew at once, as one does in dreams, who the person was. It was Jesus.

"You have been wishing that you could see me, Papa Panov." he said kindly, "then look for me tomorrow. It will be Christmas Day and I will visit you. But look carefully, for I shall not tell you who I am."

"It will be Christmas Day and I will visit you. But look carefully, for I shall not tell you who I am."

When at last Papa Panov awoke, the bells were ringing out and a thin light was filtering through the shutters. "Bless my soul!" said Papa Panov. "It's Christmas Day!"

He stood up and stretched himself for he was rather stiff. Then his face filled with happiness as he remembered his dream. This would be a very special Christmas after all, for Jesus was coming to visit him. How would he look? Would he be a little baby, as at that first Christmas? Would he be a grown man, a carpenter—or the great King that he is, God's Son? He must watch carefully the whole day through so that he recognized him however he came.

Papa Panov put on a special pot of coffee for his Christmas breakfast, took down the shutters and looked out of the window. The street was deserted, no one was stirring yet. No one except the road sweeper. He looked as miserable and dirty as ever, and well he might! Whoever wanted to work on Christmas Day—and in the raw cold and bitter freezing mist of such a morning?

Papa Panov opened the shop door, letting in a thin stream of cold air. "Come in!" he shouted across the street cheerily. "Come in and have some hot coffee to keep out the cold!"

The sweeper looked up, scarcely able to believe his ears. He was only too glad to put down his broom and come into the warm room. His old clothes steamed gently in the heat of the stove and he clasped both red hands round the comforting warm mug as he drank.

Papa Panov watched him with satisfaction, but every now and them his eyes strayed to the window. It would never do to miss his special visitor.

"Expecting someone?" the sweeper asked at last. So Papa Panov told him about his dream.

"Well, I hope he comes," the sweeper said, "you've given me a bit of Christmas cheer I never expected to have. I'd say you deserve to have your dream come true." And he actually smiled.

When he had gone, Papa Panov put on cabbage soup for his dinner, then went to the door again, scanning the street. He saw no one. But he was mistaken. Someone was coming.

The girl walked so slowly and quietly, hugging the walls of shops and houses, that it was a while before he noticed her. She looked very tired and she was carrying something. As she drew nearer he could see that it was a baby, wrapped in a thin shawl. There was such sadness in her face and in the pinched little face of the baby, that Papa Panov's heart went out to them.

"Won't you come in," he called, stepping outside to meet them. "You both need a warm seat by the fire and a rest."

The young mother let him shepherd her indoors and to the comfort of the armchair. She gave a big sigh of relief.

"I'll warm some milk for the baby," Papa Panov said, "I've had children of my own—I can feed her for you." He took the milk from the stove and carefully fed the baby from a spoon, warming her tiny feet by the stove at the same time.

"She needs shoes," the cobbler said.

But the girl replied, "I can't afford shoes, I've got no husband to bring home money. I'm on my way to the next village to get work."

A sudden thought flashed through Papa Panov's mind. He remembered the little shoes he had looked at last night. But he had been keeping those for Jesus. He looked again at the cold little feet and made up his mind.

"Try these on her," he said, handing the baby and the shoes to the mother. The beautiful little shoes were a perfect fit. The girl smiled happily and the baby gurgled with pleasure.

"You have been so kind to us," the girl said, when she got up with her baby to go. "May all your Christmas wishes come true!"

But Papa Panov was beginning to wonder if his very special Christmas wish would come true. Perhaps he had missed his visitor? He looked anxiously up and down the street. There were plenty of people about but they were all faces that he recognized. There were neighbors going to call on their families. They nodded and smiled and wished him Happy Christmas! Or beggars—and Papa Panov hurried indoors to fetch them hot soup and a generous hunk of bread, hurrying out again in case he missed the Important Stranger.

All too soon the winter dusk fell. When Papa Panov next went to the door and strained his eyes, he could no longer make out the passers-by. Most were home and indoors by now anyway. He walked slowly back into his room at last, put up the shutters, and sat down wearily in his armchair.

So it had been just a dream after all. Jesus had not come.

76

Then all at once he knew that he was no longer alone in the room.

This was not dream for he was wide awake. At first he seemed to see before his eyes the long stream of people who had come to him that day. He saw again the old road sweeper, the young mother and her baby and the beggars he had fed. As they passed, each whispered, "Didn't you see me, Papa Panov?"

"Who are you?" he called out, bewildered.

Then another voice answered him. It was the voice from his dream—the voice of Jesus.

"I was hungry and you fed me," he said. "I was naked and you clothed me. I was cold and you warmed me. I came to you today in every one of those you helped and welcomed."

Then all was quiet and still. Only the sound of the big clock ticking. A great peace and happiness seemed to fill the room, overflowing Papa Panov's heart until he wanted to burst out singing and laughing and dancing with joy.

"So he did come after all!" was all that he said.

"I was hungry and you fed me," he said. "I was naked and you clothed me. I was cold and you warmed me. I came to you today in every one of those you helped and welcomed."

—RUBEN SAILLENS (1855–1942),
translation by Leo Tolstoy (1828–1910)

Children Carrying the Wood in the Snow, Winter,
Nikolay Bogdanov-Belsky (1868–1945)

Moonless darkness stands between.
Past, the Past, no more be seen!
But the Bethlehem star may lead me
To the sight of Him Who freed me
From the self that I have been.
Make me pure, Lord: Thou art Holy;
Make me meek, Lord: Thou wert lowly;
Now beginning, and always,
Now begin, on Christmas day.

—GERARD MANLEY HOPKINS (1844–1889)

79

★ GRANT US A TRUE CHRISTMAS ★

Father of all men, look upon our family,
Kneeling together before Thee,
And grant us a true Christmas.

With loving heart we bless Thee:
For the gift of Thy dear Son Jesus Christ,
For the peace He brings to human homes,
For the good-will He teaches to sinful men,
For the glory of Thy goodness shining in His face.

With joyful voice we praise Thee:
For His lowly birth and His rest in the manger,
For the pure tenderness of His mother Mary,
For the fatherly care that protected Him,
For the Providence that saved the Holy Child
To be the Saviour of the world.

With deep desire we beseech Thee:
Help us to keep His birthday truly,
Help us to offer, in His name, our Christmas prayer.

From the sickness of sin and the darkness of doubt,
From selfish pleasures and sullen pains,
From the frost of pride and the fever of envy,
God save us every one, through the blessing of Jesus.

In the health of purity and the calm of mutual trust,
In the sharing of joy and the bearing of trouble,
In the steady glow of love and the clear light of hope,
God keep us every one, by the blessing of Jesus.

In praying and praising, in giving and receiving,

In eating and drinking, in singing and making merry,

In parents' gladness and in children's mirth,

In dear memories of those who have departed,

In good comradeship with those who are here,

In kind wishes for those who are far away,

In patient waiting, sweet contentment, generous cheer,

God bless us every one, with the blessing of Jesus.

By remembering our kinship with all men,

By well-wishing, friendly speaking and kindly doing,

By cheering the downcast and adding sunshine to daylight,

By welcoming strangers (poor shepherds or wise men),

By keeping the music of the angels' song in this home,

God help us every one to share the blessing of Jesus:

In whose name we keep Christmas:

And in whose words we pray together:

Our Father which art in heaven, hallowed be Thy name.

Thy kingdom come. Thy will be done in earth, as it is in heaven.

Give us this day our daily bread. And forgive us our debts, as we

Forgive our debtors.

And lead us not into temptation, but deliver us from evil:

For Thine is the kingdom, and the power, and the glory, forever.

Amen.

—HENRY VAN DYKE (1852–1933)

The Star of Bethlehem, Edward Burne-Jones (1833–1898)

PRESIDENTIAL MESSAGE,
★ DECEMBER 25, 1927 ★

CHRISTMAS IS NOT A TIME OR A SEASON but a state of mind. To cherish peace and good will, to be plenteous in mercy, is to have the real spirit of Christmas. If we think on these things, there will be born in us a Savior and over us will shine a star sending its gleam of hope to the world.

—CALVIN COOLIDGE (1872–1933)

83

THE SPIRIT STOOD AMONG THE GRAVES, AND POINTED down to One. Scrooge advanced towards it trembling. The Phantom was exactly as it had been, but he dreaded that he saw new meaning in its solemn shape.

"Before I draw nearer to that stone to which you point," said Scrooge, "answer me one question. Are these the shadows of the things that Will be, or are they shadows of things that May be, only?"

Still the Ghost pointed downward to the grave by which it stood.

"Men's courses will foreshadow certain ends, to which, if persevered in, they must lead," said Scrooge. "But if the courses be departed from, the ends will change. Say it is thus with what you show me!"

The Spirit was immovable as ever.

Scrooge crept towards it, trembling as he went; and following the finger, read upon the stone of the neglected grave his own name, Ebenezer Scrooge.

"Am I that man who lay upon the bed?" he cried, upon his knees.

The finger pointed from the grave to him, and back again.

"No, Spirit! Oh no, no!"

The finger still was there.

"Spirit!" he cried, tight clutching at its robe, "hear me! I am not the man I was. I will not be the man I must have been but for this intercourse. Why show me this, if I am past all hope!"

For the first time the hand appeared to shake.

"Good Spirit," he pursued, as down upon the ground he fell before it: "Your nature intercedes for me, and pities me. Assure me that I yet may change these shadows you have shown me, by an altered life!"

The kind hand trembled.

"I will honour Christmas in my heart, and try to keep it all the year. I will live in the Past, the Present, and the Future. The Spirits of all Three shall strive within me. I will not shut out the lessons that they teach. Oh, tell me I may sponge away the writing on this stone!"

In his agony, he caught the spectral hand. It sought to free itself, but he was strong in his entreaty, and detained it. The Spirit, stronger yet, repulsed him.

"I will honour Christmas in my heart,
and try to keep it all the year.
I will live in the Past, the Present,
and the Future.
The Spirits of all Three
shall strive within me.
I will not shut out the lessons
that they teach."

Holding up his hands in a last prayer to have his fate reversed, he saw an alteration in the Phantom's hood and dress. It shrunk, collapsed, and dwindled down into a bedpost.

Yes! and the bedpost was his own. The bed was his own, the room was his own. Best and happiest of all, the Time before him was his own, to make amends in!

"I will live in the Past, the Present, and the Future!" Scrooge repeated, as he scrambled out of bed. "The Spirits of all Three shall strive within me. Oh Jacob Marley! *He spoke out to his now long-deceased colleague.* Heaven, and the Christmas Time be praised for this! I say it on my knees, old Jacob, on my knees!"

He was so fluttered and so glowing with his good intentions, that his broken voice would scarcely answer to his call. He had been sobbing violently in his conflict with the Spirit, and his face was wet with tears.

"They are not torn down," cried Scrooge, folding one of his bed-curtains in his arms, "they are not torn down, rings and all. They are here

—I am here—the shadows of the things that would have been, may be dispelled. They will be. I know they will!"

His hands were busy with his garments all this time; turning them inside out, putting them on upside down, tearing them, mislaying them, making them parties to every kind of extravagance.

"I don't know what to do!" cried Scrooge, laughing and crying in the same breath; and making a perfect Laocoön of himself with his stockings. "I am as light as a feather, I am as happy as an angel, I am as merry as a schoolboy. I am as giddy as a drunken man. A merry Christmas to everybody! A happy New Year to all the world. Hallo here! Whoop! Hallo!"

He had frisked into the sitting-room, and was now standing there: perfectly winded.

"A merry Christmas to everybody! A happy New Year to all the world."

"There's the saucepan that the gruel was in!" cried Scrooge, starting off again, and going round the fireplace. "There's the door, by which the Ghost of Jacob Marley entered! There's the corner where the Ghost of Christmas Present, sat! There's the window where I saw the wandering Spirits! It's all right, it's all true, it all happened. Ha ha ha!"

Really, for a man who had been out of practice for so many years, it was a splendid laugh, a most illustrious laugh. The father of a long, long line of brilliant laughs!

"I don't know what day of the month it is!" said Scrooge. "I don't know how long I've been among the Spirits. I don't know anything. I'm quite a baby. Never mind. I don't care. I'd rather be a baby. Hallo! Whoop! Hallo here!"

He was checked in his transports by the churches ringing out the lustiest peals he had ever heard. Clash, clang, hammer; ding, dong, bell. Bell, dong, ding; hammer, clang, clash! Oh, glorious, glorious!

Running to the window, he opened it, and put out his head. No fog, no mist; clear, bright, jovial, stirring, cold; cold, piping for the blood to dance to; Golden sunlight; Heavenly sky; sweet fresh air; merry bells. Oh, glorious! Glorious!

"What's to-day!" cried Scrooge, calling downward to a boy in Sunday clothes, who perhaps had loitered in to look about him.

"EH?" returned the boy, with all his might of wonder.

"What's to-day, my fine fellow?" said Scrooge.

"To-day!" replied the boy. "Why, CHRISTMAS DAY."

"It's Christmas Day!" said Scrooge to himself. "I haven't missed it. The Spirits have done it all in one night. They can do anything they like. Of course they can. Of course they can. Hallo, my fine fellow!"

"Hallo!" returned the boy.

"Do you know the Poulterer's, in the next street but one, at the corner?" Scrooge inquired.

"I should hope I did," replied the lad.

"An intelligent boy!" said Scrooge. "A remarkable boy! Do you know whether they've sold the prize Turkey that was hanging up there? – Not the little prize Turkey: the big one?"

"What, the one as big as me?" returned the boy.

"What a delightful boy!" said Scrooge. "It's a pleasure to talk to him. Yes, my buck."

"It's hanging there now," replied the boy.

"Is it?" said Scrooge. "Go and buy it."

"Walk-ER!" exclaimed the boy.

"No, no," said Scrooge, "I am in earnest. Go and buy it, and tell 'em to bring it here, that I may give them the direction where to take it. Come back with the man, and I'll give you a shilling. Come back with him in less than five minutes and I'll give you half-a-crown!"

The boy was off like a shot. He must have had a steady hand at a trigger who could have got a shot off half so fast.

"I'll send it to my faithful, gentle clerk Bob Cratchit's!" whispered Scrooge, rubbing his hands, and splitting with a laugh. "He shan't know who sends it. It's twice the size of his son, Tiny Tim. Joe Miller never made such a joke as sending it to Bob's will be!"

The hand in which he wrote the address was not a steady one, but write it he did, somehow, and went down-stairs to open the street door, ready for the coming of the poulterer's man. As he stood there, waiting his arrival, the knocker caught his eye.

"I shall love it, as long as I live!" cried Scrooge, patting it with his hand. "I scarcely ever looked at it before. What an honest expression it has in its face! It's a wonderful knocker! – Here's the Turkey! Hallo! Whoop! How are you! Merry Christmas!"

It was a Turkey! He never could have stood upon his legs, that bird. He would have snapped 'em short off in a minute, like sticks of sealing-wax.

"Why, it's impossible to carry that to Camden Town," said Scrooge. "You must have a cab."

The chuckle with which he said this, and the chuckle with which he paid for the Turkey, and the chuckle with which he paid for the cab, and the chuckle with which he recompensed the boy, were only to be exceeded by the chuckle with which he sat down breathless in his chair again, and chuckled till he cried.

Shaving was not an easy task, for his hand continued to shake very much; and shaving requires attention, even when you don't dance while you are at it. But if he had cut the end of his nose off, he would have put a piece of sticking-plaister over it, and been quite satisfied.

He dressed himself "all in his best," and at last got out into the streets. The people were by this time pouring forth, as he had seen them with the Ghost of Christmas Present; and walking with his hands behind him, Scrooge regarded every one with a delighted smile. He looked so irresistibly pleasant, in a word, that three or four good-humoured fellows said, "Good morning, sir! A merry Christmas to you!" And Scrooge said often afterwards, that of all the blithe sounds he had ever heard, those were the blithest in his ears.

He had not gone far, when coming on towards him he beheld the portly gentleman, who had walked into his counting-house the day before, and said, "Scrooge and Marley's, I believe?" It sent a pang across his heart to think how this old gentleman would look upon him when they met; but he knew what path lay straight before him, and he took it.

"My dear sir," said Scrooge, quickening his pace, and taking the old gentleman by both his hands. "How do you do? I hope you succeeded yesterday. It was very kind of you. A merry Christmas to you, sir!"

"Mr. Scrooge?"

"Yes," said Scrooge. "That is my name, and I fear it may not be pleasant to you. Allow me to ask your pardon. And will you have the goodness" – here Scrooge whispered in his ear.

"Lord bless me!" cried the gentleman, as if his breath were taken away. "My dear Mr. Scrooge, are you serious?"

"If you please," said Scrooge. "Not a farthing less. A great many back-payments are included in it, I assure you. Will you do me that favour?"

"My dear sir," said the other, shaking hands with him. "I don't know what to say to such munifi—"

"Don't say anything, please," retorted Scrooge. "Come and see me. Will you come and see me?"

"I will!" cried the old gentleman. And it was clear he meant to do it.

"Thank you," said Scrooge. "I am much obliged to you. I thank you fifty times. Bless you!"

He went to church, and walked about the streets, and watched the people hurrying to and fro, and patted children on the head, and questioned beggars, and looked down into the kitchens of houses, and up to the windows, and found that everything could yield him pleasure. He had never dreamed that any walk – that anything – could give him so much happiness. In the afternoon he turned his steps towards his nephew's house.

He passed the door a dozen times, before he had the courage to go up and knock. But he made a dash, and did it:

"Is your master at home, my dear?" said Scrooge to the girl. Nice girl! Very.

"Yes, sir."

"Where is he, my love?" said Scrooge.

"He's in the dining-room, sir, along with mistress. I'll show you up-stairs, if you please."

"Thank'ee. He knows me," said Scrooge, with his hand already on the dining-room lock. "I'll go in here, my dear."

He turned it gently, and sidled his face in, round the door. They were looking at the table (which was spread out in great array); for these young housekeepers are always nervous on such points, and like to see that everything is right.

"Fred!" said Scrooge.

Dear heart alive, how his niece by marriage started! Scrooge had forgotten, for the moment, about her sitting in the corner with the footstool, or he wouldn't have done it, on any account.

"Why bless my soul!" cried Fred, "who's that?"

"It's I. Your uncle Scrooge. I have come to dinner. Will you let me in, Fred?"

Let him in! It is a mercy he didn't shake his arm off. He was at home in five minutes. Nothing could be heartier. His niece looked just the same. So did Topper when he came. So did the plump sister when she came. So did every one when they came. Wonderful party, wonderful games, wonderful unanimity, won-der-ful happiness!

But he was early at the office next morning. Oh, he was early there. If he could only be there first, and catch Bob Cratchit coming late! That was the thing he had set his heart upon.

And he did it; yes, he did! The clock struck nine. No Bob. A quarter past. No Bob. He was full eighteen minutes and a half behind his time. Scrooge sat with his door wide open, that he might see him come into the Tank.

His hat was off, before he opened the door; his comforter too. He was on his stool in a jiffy; driving away with his pen, as if he were trying to overtake nine o'clock.

"Hallo!" growled Scrooge, in his accustomed voice, as near as he could feign it. "What do you mean by coming here at this time of day?"

"I am very sorry, sir," said Bob. "I am behind my time."

"You are?" repeated Scrooge. "Yes. I think you are. Step this way, sir, if you please."

"It's only once a year, sir," pleaded Bob, appearing from the Tank. "It shall not be repeated. I was making rather merry yesterday, sir."

"Now, I'll tell you what, my friend," said Scrooge, "I am not going to stand this sort of thing any longer. And therefore," he continued, leaping from his stool, and giving Bob such a dig in the waistcoat that he staggered back into the Tank again; "and therefore I am about to raise your salary!"

Bob trembled, and got a little nearer to the ruler. He had a moment-ary idea of knocking Scrooge down with it, holding him, and calling to the people in the court for help and a strait-waistcoat.

"A merry Christmas, Bob," said Scrooge, with an earnestness that could not be mistaken, as he clapped him on the back. "A merrier Christmas, Bob, my good fellow, than I have given you for many a year. I'll raise your salary, and endeavour to assist your struggling family, and we will discuss your affairs this very afternoon, over a Christmas bowl of smoking bishop, Bob! Make up the fires, and buy another coal-scuttle before you dot another i, Bob Cratchit!"

"A merrier Christmas, Bob, my good fellow, than I have given you for many a year."

Scrooge was better than his word. He did it all, and infinitely more; and to Tiny Tim, he was a second father. He became as good a friend, as good a master, and as good a man, as the good old city knew, or any other good old city, town, or borough, in the good old world. Some people laughed to see the alteration in him, but he let them laugh, and little heeded them; for he was wise enough to know that nothing ever happened on this globe, for good, at which some people did not have their fill of laughter in the outset; and knowing that such as these would be blind anyway, he thought it quite as well that they should wrinkle up their eyes in grins, as have the malady in less attractive forms. His own heart laughed: and that was quite enough for him.

It was always said of him, that he knew how to keep Christmas well, if any man alive possessed the knowledge. May that be truly said of us, and all of us! And so, as Tiny Tim observed, God bless Us, Every One!

—CHARLES DICKENS (1812–1870), *A Christmas Carol*

Bob Cratchit and Tiny Tim, Jessie Willcox Smith (1863–1935)

Go, tell it on the mountain,
Over the hills and ev'rywhere;
Go, tell it on the mountain
That Jesus Christ is born.

Go, tell it on the mountain,
Over the hills and everywhere;
Go, tell it on the mountain
That Jesus Christ is born.

94

While shepherds kept their watching
O'er silent flocks by night,
Behold throughout the heavens
There shone a holy light.

Down in a lowly manger
Our humble Christ was born,
And God sent us salvation
That blessed Christmas morn.

Go, tell it on the mountain,
Over the hills and everywhere;
Go, tell it on the mountain
That Jesus Christ is born

Go, tell it on the mountain,
Over the hills and everywhere;
Go, tell it on the mountain
That Jesus Christ is born.

The shepherds feared and trembled
When lo above the Earth
Rang out the angel's chorus
That hailed our Savior's birth.

—AFRICAN-AMERICAN SPIRITUAL (ca. 1865)

W E WRITE THESE WORDS NOW, MANY MILES DISTANT from the spot at which, year after year, we met on that day, a merry and joyous circle. Many of the hearts that throbbed so gaily then, have ceased to beat; many of the looks that shone so brightly then, have ceased to glow; the hands we grasped, have grown cold; the eyes we sought, have hid their lustre in the grave; and yet the old house, the room, the merry voices and smiling faces, the jest, the laugh, the most minute and trivial circumstances connected with those happy meetings, crowd upon our mind at each recurrence of the season, as if the last assemblage had been but yesterday!

Happy, happy Christmas, that can win us back to the delusions of our childish days; that can recall to the old man the pleasures of his youth; that can transport the sailor and the traveller, thousands of miles away, back to his own fireside and his quiet home!

—CHARLES DICKENS (1812–1870), *The Pickwick Papers*

Two Angels, Follower of Giotto (ca. 1328)

Meadow with Pine Trees, Ivan Shishkin (1832–1898)

O<small>NCE UPON A TIME THE FOREST WAS IN A GREAT</small> commotion. Early in the evening the wise old cedars had shaken their heads ominously and predicted strange things. They had lived in the forest many, many years; but never had they seen such marvelous sights as were to be seen now in the sky, and upon the hills, and in the distant village.

"Pray tell us what you see," pleaded a little vine; "we who are not as tall as you can behold none of these wonderful things. Describe them to us, that we may enjoy them with you."

"I am filled with such amazement," said one of the cedars, "that I can hardly speak. The whole sky seems to be aflame, and the stars appear to be dancing among the clouds; angels walk down from heaven to the earth, and enter the village or talk with the shepherds upon the hills."

The vine listened in mute astonishment. Such things never before had happened. The vine trembled with excitement. Its nearest neighbor was a tiny tree, so small it scarcely ever was noticed; yet it was a very beautiful little tree, and the vines and ferns and mosses and other humble residents of the forest loved it dearly.

"How I should like to see the angels!" sighed the little tree, "and how I should like to see the stars dancing among the clouds! It must be very beautiful."

As the vine and the little tree talked of these things, the cedars watched with increasing interest the wonderful scenes over and beyond the confines of the forest. Presently they thought they heard music, and they were not mistaken, for soon the whole air was full of the sweetest harmonies ever heard upon earth.

"What beautiful music!" cried the little tree. "I wonder whence it comes."

"The angels are singing," said a cedar; "for none but angels could make such sweet music."

"But the stars are singing, too," said another cedar; "yes, and the shepherds on the hills join in the song, and what a strangely glorious song it is!"

The trees listened to the singing, but they did not understand its meaning: it seemed to be an anthem, and it was of a Child that had been born; but further than this they did not understand. The strange and glorious song continued all the night; and all that night the angels walked to and fro, and the shepherd-folk talked with the angels, and the stars danced and caroled in high heaven.

And it was nearly morning when the cedars cried out, "They are coming to the forest! the angels are coming to the forest!" And, surely enough, this was true. The vine and the little tree were very terrified, and they begged their older and stronger neighbors to protect them from harm. But the cedars were too busy with their own fears to pay any heed to the faint pleadings of the humble vine and the little tree.

The angels came into the forest, singing the same glorious anthem about the Child, and the stars sang in chorus with them, until every part of the woods rang with echoes of that wondrous song. There was nothing in the appearance of this angel host to inspire fear; they were clad all in white, and there were crowns upon their fair heads, and golden harps in their hands; love, hope, charity, compassion, and joy beamed from their beautiful faces, and their presence seemed to fill the forest with a divine peace.

The angels came through the forest to where the little tree stood, and gathering around it, they touched it with their hands, and kissed its little branches, and sang even more sweetly than before. And their song was about the Child, the Child, the Child that had been born.

Then the stars came down from the skies and danced and hung upon the branches of the tree, and they, too, sang that song,—the song of the Child. And all the other trees and the vines and the ferns and the mosses beheld in wonder; nor could they understand why all these things were being done, and why this exceeding honor should be shown the little tree.

When the morning came the angels left the forest,—all but one angel, who remained behind and lingered near the little tree. Then a cedar asked: "Why do you tarry with us, holy angel?" And the angel answered: "I stay to guard this little tree, for it is sacred, and no harm shall come to it."

The little tree felt quite relieved by this assurance, and it held up its head more confidently than ever before. And how it thrived and grew, and waxed in strength and beauty! The cedars said they never had seen the like. The sun seemed to lavish its choicest rays upon the little tree, heaven dropped its sweetest dew upon it, and the winds never came to the forest that they did not forget their rude manners and linger to kiss the little tree and sing it their prettiest songs. No danger ever menaced it, no harm threatened; for the angel never slept,—through the day and through the night the angel watched the little tree and protected it from all evil. Oftentimes the trees talked with the angel; but of course they understood little of what he said, for he spoke always of the Child who was to become the Master; and always when thus he talked, he caressed the little tree, and stroked its branches and leaves, and moistened them with his tears. It all was so very strange that none in the forest could understand.

So the years passed, the angel watching his blooming charge. Sometimes the beasts strayed toward the little tree and threatened to devour its tender foliage; sometimes the woodman came with his axe, intent upon hewing down the straight and comely thing; sometimes the hot, consuming breath of drought swept from the south, and sought to blight the forest and all its verdure: the angel kept them from the little tree. Serene and beautiful it grew, until now it was no longer a little tree, but the pride and glory of the forest.

One day the tree heard some one coming through the forest. Hitherto the angel had hastened to its side when men approached; but now the angel strode away and stood under the cedars yonder.

"Dear angel," cried the tree, "can you not hear the footsteps of some one approaching? Why do you leave me?"

"Have no fear," said the angel; "for He who comes is the Master."

The Master came to the tree and beheld it. He placed His hands upon its smooth trunk and branches, and the tree was thrilled with a strange and glorious delight. Then He stooped and kissed the tree, and then He turned and went away.

Many times after that the Master came to the forest, and when He came it always was to where the tree stood. Many times He rested beneath the tree and enjoyed the shade of its foliage, and listened to the music of the wind as it swept through the rustling leaves. Many times He slept there, and the tree watched over Him, and the forest was still, and all its voices were hushed. And the angel hovered near like a faithful sentinel.

Ever and anon men came with the Master to the forest, and sat with Him in the shade of the tree, and talked with Him of matters which the tree never could understand; only it heard that the talk was of love and charity and gentleness, and it saw that the Master was beloved and venerated by the others. It heard them tell of the Master's goodness and humility,—how He had healed the sick and raised the dead and bestowed inestimable blessings wherever He walked. And the tree loved the Master for His beauty and His goodness; and when He came to the forest it was full of joy, but when He came not it was sad. And the other

100

trees of the forest joined in its happiness and its sorrow, for they, too, loved the Master. And the angel always hovered near.

The Master came one night alone into the forest, and His face was pale with anguish and wet with tears, and He fell upon His knees and prayed. The tree heard Him, and all the forest was still, as if it were standing in the presence of death. And when the morning came, lo! the angel had gone.

Then there was a great confusion in the forest. There was a sound of rude voices, and a clashing of swords and staves. Strange men appeared, uttering loud oaths and cruel threats, and the tree was filled with terror. It called aloud for the angel, but the angel came not.

"Alas," cried the vine, "they have come to destroy the tree, the pride and glory of the forest!"

The forest was sorely agitated, but it was in vain. The strange men plied their axes with cruel vigor, and the tree was hewn to the ground. Its beautiful branches were cut away and cast aside, and its soft, thick foliage was strewn to the tenderer mercies of the winds.

"They are killing me!" cried the tree; "why is not the angel here to protect me?"

But no one heard the piteous cry,—none but the other trees of the forest; and they wept, and the little vine wept too.

Then the cruel men dragged the despoiled and hewn tree from the forest, and the forest saw that beauteous thing no more.

But the night wind that swept down from the City of the Great King that night to ruffle the bosom of distant Galilee, tarried in the forest awhile to say that it had seen that day a cross upraised on Calvary,—the tree on which was stretched the body of the dying Master.

—Eugene Field (1850–1895),
Christmas Tales and Christmas Verse

Three Kings came riding from far away,
Melchior and Gaspar and Baltasar;
Three Wise Men out of the East were they,
And they travelled by night and they slept by day,
For their guide was a beautiful, wonderful star.

The star was so beautiful, large and clear,
That all the other stars of the sky
Became a white mist in the atmosphere,
And by this they knew that the coming was near
Of the Prince foretold in the prophecy

Three caskets they bore on their saddle-bows,
Three caskets of gold with golden keys;
Their robes were of crimson silk with rows
Of bells and pomegranates and furbelows,
Their turbans like blossoming almond-trees.

And so the Three Kings rode into the West,
Through the dusk of the night, over hill and dell,
And sometimes they nodded with beard on breast,
And sometimes talked, as they paused to rest,
With the people they met at some wayside well.

"Of the child that is born," said Baltasar,
"Good people, I pray you, tell us the news;
For we in the East have seen his star,
And have ridden fast, and have ridden far,
To find and worship the King of the Jews."

And the people answered, "You ask in vain;
We know of no King but Herod the Great!"
They thought the Wise Men were men insane,
As they spurred their horses across the plain,
Like riders in haste, who cannot wait.

And when they came to Jerusalem,
Herod the Great, who had heard this thing,
Sent for the Wise Men and questioned them;
And said, "Go down unto Bethlehem,
And bring me tidings of this new king."

So they rode away; and the star stood still,
The only one in the grey of morn;
Yes, it stopped—it stood still of its own free will,
Right over Bethlehem on the hill,
The city of David, where Christ was born.

And the Three Kings rode through the gate and the guard,
Through the silent street, till their horses turned
And neighed as they entered the great inn-yard;
But the windows were closed, and the doors were barred,
And only a light in the stable burned.

And cradled there in the scented hay,
In the air made sweet by the breath of kine,
The little child in the manger lay,
The child, that would be king one day
Of a kingdom not human, but divine.

His mother Mary of Nazareth
Sat watching beside his place of rest,
Watching the even flow of his breath,
For the joy of life and the terror of death
Were mingled together in her breast.

They laid their offerings at his feet:
The gold was their tribute to a King,
The frankincense, with its odor sweet,
Was for the Priest, the Paraclete,
The myrrh for the body's burying.

And the mother wondered and bowed her head,
And sat as still as a statue of stone,
Her heart was troubled yet comforted,
Remembering what the Angel had said
Of an endless reign and of David's throne.

Then the Kings rode out of the city gate,
With a clatter of hoofs in proud array;
But they went not back to Herod the Great,
For they knew his malice and feared his hate,
And returned to their homes by another way.

—HENRY WADSWORTH LONGFELLOW (1807–1882)

The Adoration of the Magi, Neapolitan Follower of Giotto
(ca. 1340–43)

The kings they came from out the south,
All dressed in ermine fine,
They bore Him gold and chrysoprase,
And gifts of precious wine.

106

The shepherds came from out the north,
Their coats were brown and old,
They brought Him little new-born lambs—
They had not any gold.

The wise-men came from out the east,
And they were wrapped in white;
The star that led them all the way
Did glorify the night.

The angels came from heaven high,
And they were clad with wings;
And lo, they brought a joyful song
The host of heaven sings.

The kings they knocked upon the door,
The wise-men entered in,
The shepherds followed after them
To hear the song begin.

And Mary held the little child
And sat upon the ground;
She looked up, she looked down,
She looked all around.

The angels sang thro' all the night
Until the rising sun,
But little Jesus fell asleep
Before the song was done.

—SARA TEASDALE (1884–1933)

The time draws near the birth of Christ;
The moon is hid—the night is still;
The Christmas bells from hill to hill
Answer each other in the mist.

108

Four voices of four hamlets round,
From far and near, on mead and moor,
Swell out and fail, as if a door
Were shut between me and the sound.

Each voice four changes on the wind,
That now dilate and now decrease,
Peace and good-will, good-will and peace,
Peace and good-will to all mankind.

Rise, happy morn! rise, holy morn!
Draw forth the cheerful day from night;
O Father! touch the east, and light
The light that shone when hope was born!

—ALFRED, LORD TENNYSON (1809–1892)

A Christmas Carol, Dante Gabriel Rossetti (1828–1882)

I heard the bells on Christmas Day
Their old, familiar carols play,
And wild and sweet
The words repeat
Of peace on earth, good-will to men!

And thought how, as the day had come,
The belfries of all Christendom
Had rolled along
The unbroken song
Of peace on earth, good-will to men!

Till ringing, singing on its way,
The world revolved from night to day,
A voice, a chime,
A chant sublime
Of peace on earth, good-will to men!

Then from each black, accursed mouth
The cannon thundered in the South,
And with the sound
The carols drowned
Of peace on earth, good-will to men!

It was as if an earthquake rent
The hearth-stones of a continent,
And made forlorn
The households born
Of peace on earth, good-will to men!

And in despair I bowed my head;
"There is no peace on earth," I said;
"For hate is strong,
And mocks the song
Of peace on earth, good-will to men!"

Then pealed the bells more loud and deep:
"God is not dead, nor doth He sleep;
The Wrong shall fail,
The Right prevail,
With peace on earth, good-will to men."

—HENRY WADSWORTH LONGFELLOW (1807–1882)

111

The Nativity, © Adobe Stock

LOVE CAME DOWN
★ AT CHRISTMAS ★

Love came down at Christmas,
Love all lovely, Love Divine,
Love was born at Christmas,
Star and Angels gave the sign.
Worship we the Godhead,
Love Incarnate, Love Divine,
Worship we our Jesus,
But wherewith for sacred sign?
Love shall be our token,
Love be yours and love be mine,
Love to God and all men,
Love for plea and gift and sign.

—CHRISTINA ROSSETTI (1830–1894)

There fared a mother driven forth
Out of an inn to roam;
In the place where she was homeless
All men are at home.
The crazy stable close at hand,
With shaking timber and shifting sand,
Grew a stronger thing to abide and stand
Than the square stones of Rome.

For men are homesick in their homes,
And strangers under the sun,
And they lay on their heads in a foreign land
Whenever the day is done.
Here we have battle and blazing eyes,
And chance and honour and high surprise,
But our homes are under miraculous skies
Where the yule tale was begun.

A Child in a foul stable,
Where the beasts feed and foam;
Only where He was homeless
Are you and I at home;
We have hands that fashion and heads that know,
But our hearts we lost – how long ago!
In a place no chart nor ship can show
Under the sky's dome.

This world is wild as an old wives' tale,
And strange the plain things are,
The earth is enough and the air is enough
For our wonder and our war;
But our rest is as far as the fire-drake swings
And our peace is put in impossible things
Where clashed and thundered unthinkable wings
Round an incredible star.

To an open house in the evening
Home shall men come,
To an older place than Eden
And a taller town than Rome.
To the end of the way of the wandering star,
To the things that cannot be and that are,
To the place where God was homeless
And all mortals are at home.

—G. K. Chesterton (1874–1936)

Most high, all powerful, all good Lord!
All praise is yours, all glory, all honor, and all blessing.
To you, alone, Most High, do they belong.
No mortal lips are worthy to pronounce your name.
Be praised, my Lord, through all your creatures,
especially through my lord Brother Sun,
who brings the day; and you give light through him.
And he is beautiful and radiant in all his splendor!
Of you, Most High, he bears the likeness.
Be praised, my Lord, through Sister Moon and the stars;
in the heavens you have made them bright, precious and beautiful.

Be praised, my Lord, through Brothers Wind and Air,
and clouds and storms, and all the weather,
through which you give your creatures sustenance.
Be praised, My Lord, through Sister Water;
she is very useful, and humble, and precious, and pure.
Be praised, my Lord, through Brother Fire,
through whom you brighten the night.
He is beautiful and cheerful, and powerful and strong.
Be praised, my Lord, through our sister Mother Earth,
who feeds us and rules us,
and produces various fruits with colored flowers and herbs.

Be praised, my Lord, through those who forgive for love of you;
through those who endure sickness and trial.
Happy those who endure in peace,
for by you, Most High, they will be crowned.
Be praised, my Lord, through our Sister Bodily Death,
from whose embrace no living person can escape.
Woe to those who die in mortal sin!
Happy those she finds doing your most holy will.
The second death can do no harm to them.
Praise and bless my Lord, and give thanks,
and serve him with great humility.

—St. Francis of Assisi (ca. 1181–1226)

The Sun, Edvard Munch (1863–1944)

THE HOPE
✶ OF ALL THAT BREATHES ✶

On our way to the woods my dog veered left, off the path. I've learned that following her, on days I'm awake, leads to revelation. She brought me to a small manger made of new wood freshly sawed and nailed together. Made in the traditional Nativity-scene shape, the manger had been placed at the edge of the woods. It was empty.

I suspected the four children living in the house nearby. Outdoors often, aided by their parents, they play games in the woods involving light sabers, capes, and crowns. They are still seers.

The manger appeared a week into Advent. Brittle brown leaves from the oak above blew into and out of it. Then one day the manger was not empty. It was filled to the brim with hay. Two days later the hay had been dumped onto the ground and the manger moved a few feet away. It was now half full of shelled corn. A single fox squirrel sat up in the manger, leisurely eating kernel after kernel.

I found the children pulling each other through the snow on sleds. "Tell me about the manger," I said.

The oldest, a boy, said, "It's for the deer. We like to watch them. Next we're going to put a hunk of salt..."

The smallest, a girl, who had her head tipped back, mouth open to taste the falling flakes, interrupted. "It's for *all* the animals."

In the fullness of time, the Christmas story says, a girl gave birth ringed by animals. She lay the baby in one of their feeding troughs where animal bodies would warm the air around his fresh-born human body. Mother and child fell asleep and woke to their chuffs and shuffling hooves, their calls and the shuddering of their hides. Later sheep herders smelling of dirt, damp wool, and milk crowded into the stable. Out in the wild night fields these animal men sitting in the dark were the first to get the word. A baby had been born, they were told, who would show people a way out of their small pinched lives, a way to abandon themselves to the ever-present, unstoppable current of Love that carries all things to radiant wholeness. To recognize him they should look for a child at home among animals.

At the edge of the woods where children put out corn and salt and watch for them, and name them and speak to them, the animals wait. Will they one day find the manger empty, the children indoors?

So much rushes children to drop their capes and crowns in the leaf-meal, so much clamors and flashes for their attention. As they grow, will they lose the sight that sees light and spirit in other creatures? Or will they, despite the rush and clamor, find irresistible the beauty quietly radiating from everything that is?

To the animals it makes all the difference.
Their hope, and the hope of all that breathes, is that human
ones abandon themselves to the One Great Love.
For that, all creation waits.

—GAYLE BOSS (1957–), from *All Creation Waits*

Ring out, wild bells, to the wild sky,
　The flying cloud, the frosty light:
　The year is dying in the night;
Ring out, wild bells, and let him die.

Ring out the old, ring in the new,
　Ring, happy bells, across the snow:
　The year is going, let him go;
Ring out the false, ring in the true.

Ring out the grief that saps the mind
　For those that here we see no more;
　Ring out the feud of rich and poor,
Ring in redress to all mankind.

Ring out a slowly dying cause,
　And ancient forms of party strife;
　Ring in the nobler modes of life,
With sweeter manners, purer laws.

Ring out the want, the care, the sin,
　The faithless coldness of the times;
　Ring out, ring out my mournful rhymes
But ring the fuller minstrel in.

Ring out false pride in place and blood,
　The civic slander and the spite;
　Ring in the love of truth and right,
Ring in the common love of good.

Ring out old shapes of foul disease;
   Ring out the narrowing lust of gold;
   Ring out the thousand wars of old,
Ring in the thousand years of peace.

Ring in the valiant man and free,
   The larger heart, the kindlier hand;
   Ring out the darkness of the land,
Ring in the Christ that is to be.

—ALFRED, LORD TENNYSON (1809–1892)

121

THOU MUST LEAVE THY
★ LOWLY DWELLING ★

Thou must leave thy lowly dwelling,
The humble crib, the stable bare,
Babe, all mortal babes excelling,
Content our earthly lot to share,
Loving father, loving mother,
Shelter thee with tender care!

Blessed Jesus, we implore thee
With humble love and holy fear,
In the land that lies before thee,
Forget not us who linger here!
May the shepherd's lowly calling
Ever to thy heart be dear!

Blest are ye beyond all measure,
Thou happy father, mother mild!
Guard ye well your heavn'ly treasure,
The Prince of Peace, the Holy Child!
God go with you, God protect you,
Guide you safely through the wild!

—HECTOR BERLIOZ (1803–1869), translation by Paul England

*Our hearts grow tender with childhood memories and
love of kindred, and we are better
throughout the year for having, in spirit,
become a child again at Christmastime.*

—Laura Ingalls Wilder (1867–1957)

The Monet Family in Their Garden at Argenteuil, Edouard Manet (1832–1883)

THE DAY SHALL DAWN
✶ UPON US ✶

"Blessed be the Lord God of Israel,

for he has visited and redeemed his people,

and has raised up a horn of salvation for us

in the house of his servant David.

And you, child, will be called the prophet of the Most High;

for you will go before the Lord to prepare his ways,

to give knowledge of salvation to his people

in the forgiveness of their sins,

through the tender mercy of our God,

when the day shall dawn upon us from on high

to give light to those who sit in darkness and in the shadow of death,

to guide our feet into the way of peace."

—LUKE 1:68–79 (RSV), ADAPTED

Landscape with Green Trees or Beech Trees in Kerduel, Maurice Dennis (1870–1943)

Cold and wintry is the sky,
  Bitter winds go whistling by,
  Orchard boughs are bare and dry,
Yet here stands a fruitful tree.
  Household fairies kind and dear,
  With loving magic none need fear,
  Bade it rise and blossom here,
Little friends, for you and me.

Come and gather as they fall,
  Shining gifts for great and small;
  Santa Claus remembers all
When he comes with goodies piled.
  Corn and candy, apples red,
  Sugar horses, gingerbread,
  Creatures that need not be fed,
Are hanging here for every child.

Shake the boughs and down they come,
Better fruit than peach or plum,
'Tis our little harvest home;
For though frosts the flowers kill,
Though birds depart and squirrels sleep,
Though snows may gather cold and deep,
Little folk their sunshine keep,
And mother-love makes summer still.

Gathered in a smiling ring,
Lightly dance and gayly sing,
Still at heart remembering
The sweet story all should know,
Of the little Child whose birth
Has made this day throughout the earth
A festival for childish mirth,
Since that first Christmas long ago.

—LOUISA MAY ALCOTT (1832–1888), ADAPTED

Three Magi, Cesare Nebbia (ca. 1536–ca. 1622)

WHEN THEY SAW THE STAR, they rejoiced with exceedingly great joy. And when they had come into the house, they saw the young Child with Mary His mother, and fell down and worshiped Him. And when they had opened their treasures, they presented gifts to Him: gold, frankincense, and myrrh.

—MATTHEW 2:10–11 (NKJV)

★ THE WISE MEN ★

Step softly, under snow or rain,
    To find the place where all can pray;
The way is all so very plain
    That we may lose the way.

Oh, we have learnt to peer and pore
    On tortured puzzles from our youth,
We know all the labyrinthine lore,
We are the three wise men of yore,
    And we know all things but the truth.

We have gone round and round the hill
    And lost the wood among the trees,
And learnt long names for every ill,
And serve the made gods, naming still
    The Furies the Eumenides.

The gods of violence took the veil
    Of vision and philosophy,
The Serpent that brought all men bale,
He bites his own accursed tail,
    And calls himself Eternity.

Go humbly ... it has hailed and snowed ...
    With voices low and lanterns lit;
So very simple is the road,
    That we may stray from it.

The world grows terrible and white,
　　And blinding white the breaking day;
We walk bewildered in the light,
For something is too large for sight,
　　And something much too plain to say.

The Child that was ere worlds begun
　　(. . . We need but walk a little way,
We need but see a latch undone . . .)
The Child that played with moon and sun
　　Is playing with a little hay.

The house from which the heavens are fed,
　　The old strange house that is our own,
Where trick of words are never said,
And Mercy is as plain as bread,
　　And Honour is as hard as stone.

Go humbly, humble are the skies,
　　And low and large and fierce the Star;
So very near the Manger lies
　　That we may travel far.

Hark! Laughter like a lion wakes
　　To roar to the resounding plain.
And the whole heaven shouts and shakes,
　　For God Himself is born again,
And we are little children walking
　　Through the snow and rain.

　　　　—G. K. Chesterton (1874–1936)

The Adoration of the Magi, Pedro Atanasio Bocanegra (1638–1688)

Saw you never in the twilight,
   When the sun had left the skies,
Up in heaven the clear stars shining,
   Through the gloom like silver eyes?
So of old the wise men watching,
   Saw a little stranger star,
And they knew the King was given,
   And they follow'd it from far.

Heard you never of the story,
   How they cross'd the desert wild,
Journey'd on by plain and mountain,
   Till they found the Holy Child?
How they open'd all their treasure,
   Kneeling to that Infant King,
Gave the gold and fragrant incense,
   Gave the myrrh in offering?

Know ye not that lowly Baby
   Was the bright and morning star,
He who came to light the Gentiles,
   And the darken'd isles afar?
And we too may seek his cradle,
   There our heart's best treasures bring,
Love, and Faith, and true devotion,
   For our Saviour, God, and King.

—CECIL FRANCES ALEXANDER (1818–1895)

ONE DOLLAR AND EIGHTY-SEVEN CENTS. THAT WAS ALL. And sixty cents of it was in pennies. Pennies saved one and two at a time by bulldozing the grocer and the vegetable man and the butcher until one's cheeks burned with the silent imputation of parsimony that such close dealing implied. Three times Della counted it. One dollar and eighty-seven cents. And the next day would be Christmas.

There was clearly nothing to do but flop down on the shabby little couch and howl. So Della did it. Which instigates the moral reflection that life is made up of sobs, sniffles, and smiles, with sniffles predominating.

While the mistress of the home is gradually subsiding from the first stage to the second, take a look at the home. A furnished flat at $8 per week. It did not exactly beggar description, but it certainly had that word on the lookout for the mendicancy squad.

In the vestibule below was a letter-box into which no letter would go, and an electric button from which no mortal finger could coax a ring. Also appertaining thereunto was a card bearing the name "Mr. James Dillingham Young."

The "Dillingham" had been flung to the breeze during a former period of prosperity when its possessor was being paid $30 per week. Now, when the income was shrunk to $20, the letters of "Dillingham" looked blurred, as though they were thinking seriously of contracting to a modest and unassuming D. But whenever Mr. James Dillingham Young came home and reached his flat above he was called "Jim" and greatly hugged by Mrs. James Dillingham Young, already introduced to you as Della. Which is all very good.

Della finished her cry and attended to her cheeks with the powder rag. She stood by the window and looked out dully at a gray cat walking a gray fence in a gray backyard. Tomorrow would be Christmas Day, and she had only $1.87 with which to buy Jim a present. She had been saving every penny she could for months, with this result. Twenty dollars a week doesn't go far. Expenses had been greater than she had calculated. They always are. Only $1.87 to buy a present for Jim. Her Jim. Many a happy hour she had spent planning for something nice for him. Something fine and rare and sterling—something just a little bit near to being worthy of the honor of being owned by Jim.

Many a happy hour she had spent planning for something nice for him. Something fine and rare and sterling—something just a little bit near to being worthy of the honor of being owned by Jim.

There was a pier-glass between the windows of the room. Perhaps you have seen a pier-glass in an $8 flat. A very thin and very agile person may, by observing his reflection in a rapid sequence of longitudinal strips, obtain a fairly accurate conception of his looks. Della, being slender, had mastered the art.

Suddenly she whirled from the window and stood before the glass. Her eyes were shining brilliantly, but her face had lost its color within twenty seconds. Rapidly she pulled down her hair and let it fall to its full length.

Now, there were two possessions of the James Dillingham Youngs in which they both took a mighty pride. One was Jim's gold watch that had been his father's and his grandfather's. The other was Della's hair. Had the Queen of Sheba lived in the flat across the airshaft, Della would have let her hair hang out the window some day to dry just to depreciate Her Majesty's jewels and gifts. Had King Solomon been the janitor, with all his treasures piled up in the basement, Jim would have pulled out his watch every time he passed, just to see him pluck at his beard from envy.

So now Della's beautiful hair fell about her, rippling and shining like a cascade of brown waters. It reached below her knee and made itself almost a garment for her. And then she did it up again nervously and quickly. Once she faltered for a minute and stood still while a tear or two splashed on the worn red carpet.

On went her old brown jacket; on went her old brown hat. With a whirl of skirts and with the brilliant sparkle still in her eyes, she fluttered out the door and down the stairs to the street.

Where she stopped the sign read: "Mme. Sofronie. Hair Goods of All Kinds." One flight up Della ran, and collected herself, panting. Madame, large, too white, chilly, hardly looked the "Sofronie."

"Will you buy my hair?" asked Della.

"I buy hair," said Madame. "Take yer hat off and let's have a sight at the looks of it."

Down rippled the brown cascade. "Twenty dollars," said Madame, lifting the mass with a practised hand.

"Give it to me quick," said Della.

Oh, and the next two hours tripped by on rosy wings. Forget the hashed metaphor. She was ransacking the stores for Jim's present.

She found it at last. It surely had been made for Jim and no one else. There was no other like it in any of the stores, and she had turned all of them inside out. It was a platinum fob chain simple and chaste in design, properly proclaiming its value by substance alone and not by meretricious ornamentation—as all good things should do. It was even worthy of The Watch. As soon as she saw it she knew that it must be Jim's. It was like him. Quietness and value—the description applied to both. Twenty-one dollars they took from her for it, and she hurried home with the 87 cents. With that chain on his watch Jim might be properly anxious about the time in any company. Grand as the watch was, he sometimes looked at it on the sly on account of the old leather strap that he used in place of a chain.

When Della reached home her intoxication gave way a little to prudence and reason. She got out her curling irons and lighted the gas and went to work repairing the ravages made by generosity added to love. Which is always a tremendous task, dear friends—a mammoth task.

Within forty minutes her head was covered with tiny, close-lying curls that made her look wonderfully like a truant schoolboy. She looked at her reflection in the mirror long, carefully, and critically.

"If Jim doesn't kill me," she said to herself, "before he takes a second look at me, he'll say I look like a Coney Island chorus girl. But what could I do—oh! what could I do with a dollar and eighty-seven cents?"

At 7 o'clock the coffee was made and the frying-pan was on the back of the stove hot and ready to cook the chops.

Jim was never late. Della doubled the fob chain in her hand and sat on the corner of the table near the door that he always entered. Then she heard his step on the stair away down on the first flight, and she turned white for just a moment. She had a habit for saying little silent prayers about the simplest everyday things, and now she whispered: "Please God, make him think I am still pretty."

The door opened and Jim stepped in and closed it. He looked thin and very serious. Poor fellow, he was only twenty-two—and to be burdened with a family! He needed a new overcoat and he was without gloves.

Jim stopped inside the door, as immovable as a setter at the scent of quail. His eyes were fixed upon Della, and there was an expression in them that she could not read, and it terrified her. It was not anger, nor surprise, nor disapproval, nor horror, nor any of the sentiments that she had been prepared for. He simply stared at her fixedly with that peculiar expression on his face.

Della wriggled off the table and went for him.

"Jim, darling," she cried, "don't look at me that way. I had my hair cut off and sold because I couldn't have lived through Christmas without giving you a present. It'll grow out again—you won't mind, will you? I just had to do it. My hair grows awfully fast. Say 'Merry Christmas!' Jim, and let's be happy. You don't know what a nice—what a beautiful, nice gift I've got for you."

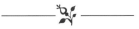

It was not anger, nor surprise, nor disapproval, nor horror, nor any of the sentiments that she had been prepared for. He simply stared at her fixedly with that peculiar expression on his face.

"You've cut off your hair?" asked Jim, laboriously, as if he had not arrived at that patent fact yet even after the hardest mental labor.

"Cut it off and sold it," said Della. "Don't you like me just as well, anyhow? I'm me without my hair, ain't I?"

Jim looked about the room curiously.

"You say your hair is gone?" he said, with an air almost of idiocy.

"You needn't look for it," said Della. "It's sold, I tell you—sold and gone, too. It's Christmas Eve, boy. Be good to me, for it went for you. Maybe the hairs of my head were numbered," she went on with sudden serious sweetness, "but nobody could ever count my love for you. Shall I put the chops on, Jim?"

Out of his trance Jim seemed quickly to wake. He enfolded his Della. For ten seconds let us regard with discreet scrutiny some inconsequential object in the other direction. Eight dollars a week or a million a year— what is the difference? A mathematician or a wit would give you the wrong answer. The magi brought valuable gifts, but that was not among them. This dark assertion will be illuminated later on.

Jim drew a package from his overcoat pocket and threw it upon the table.

"Don't make any mistake, Dell," he said, "about me. I don't think there's anything in the way of a haircut or a shave or a shampoo that could make me like my girl any less. But if you'll unwrap that package you may see why you had me going a while at first."

White fingers and nimble tore at the string and paper. And then an ecstatic scream of joy; and then, alas! a quick feminine change to hysterical tears and wails, necessitating the immediate employment of all the comforting powers of the lord of the flat.

For there lay The Combs—the set of combs, side and back, that Della had worshipped long in a Broadway window. Beautiful combs, pure tortoise shell, with jeweled rims—just the shade to wear in the beautiful vanished hair. They were expensive combs, she knew, and her heart had simply craved and yearned over them without the least hope of possession. And now, they were hers, but the tresses that should have adorned the coveted adornments were gone.

But she hugged them to her bosom, and at length she was able to look up with dim eyes and a smile and say: "My hair grows so fast, Jim!"

And then Della leaped up like a little singed cat and cried, "Oh, oh!"

Jim had not yet seen his beautiful present. She held it out to him eagerly upon her open palm. The dull precious metal seemed to flash with a reflection of her bright and ardent spirit.

"Isn't it a dandy, Jim? I hunted all over town to find it. You'll have to look at the time a hundred times a day now. Give me your watch. I want to see how it looks on it."

Instead of obeying, Jim tumbled down on the couch and put his hands under the back of his head and smiled.

"Dell," said he, "let's put our Christmas presents away and keep 'em a while. They're too nice to use just at present. I sold the watch to get the money to buy your combs. And now suppose you put the chops on."

The magi, as you know, were wise men— wonderfully wise men—who brought gifts to the Babe in the manger. They invented the art of giving Christmas presents. Being wise, their gifts were no doubt wise ones, possibly bearing the privilege of exchange in case of duplication. And here I have lamely related to you the uneventful chronicle of two foolish children in a flat who most unwisely sacrificed for each other the greatest treasures of their house. But in a last word to the wise of these days let it be said that of all who give gifts these two were the wisest. Of all who give and receive gifts, such as they are wisest. Everywhere they are wisest. They are the magi.

*Of all who give
and receive gifts,
such as they are wisest.
Everywhere they are wisest.
They are the magi.*

—O. Henry (1862–1910)

✦ SOURCES ✦

Afanasyev, Alexander Nikolaevich. *Russian Folk-Tales*. Translated by Leonard Arthur Magnus. New York: E. P. Dutton & Company, 1916.

Alcott, Louisa May. *Little Women, or, Meg, Jo, Beth, and Amy*. Boston, MA: Roberts Bros., 1880.

Dickens, Charles. *A Christmas Carol: In Prose: A Ghost Story of Christmas*. London: Chapman & Hall, 1870.

Dickens, Charles. *The Pickwick Papers*. London: Chapman and Hall, 1837.

Field, Eugene. *Christmas Tales And Christmas Verse*. New York: Charles Scribner's Sons, 1912.

Grimes, Nikki. *Glory in the Margins: Sunday Poems*. Brewster, MA: Paraclete Press, 2021.

Grün, Anselm. *Your Light Gives Us Hope: 24 Daily Practices for Advent*. Brewster, MA: Paraclete Press, 2017.

Merton, Thomas. *Raids on the Unspeakable: Prose Writing*. New York: New Directions, 1966.

Pennoyer, Greg. *God with Us: Rediscovering the Meaning of Christmas*. Brewster, MA: Paraclete Press, 2015.

Shaw, Luci. *The Generosity: Poems*. Brewster, MA: Paraclete Press, 2020.

Steven, Kenneth C. *Iona: New and Selected Poems*. Brewster, MA: Paraclete Press, 2021.

Villano, Mark A. *Time to Get Ready: An Advent, Christmas Reader to Wake Your Soul*. Brewster, MA: Paraclete Press, 2015.

SEASON *of* BEAUTY

A LENT AND EASTER TREASURY OF READINGS, ◆ POEMS, AND PRAYERS ◆

www.paracletepress.com